USBORNE HOTSHOTS

UFOs

USBORNE HOTSHOTS

UFOs

Edited by Caroline Young
Designed by Karen Tomlins

Series editor: Judy Tatchell
Series designer: Ruth Russell

Illustrated by Mike Baber, Roland Berry, Gary Bines, Kim Blundell, Derek Bunce, Kuo Kang Chen, Gordon Davies, John Francis, Terry Hadler, Graham Humphreys, John Marshall, Gary Mayes, Martin Newton, Mike Pringle, Chris Reed, Michael Roffe and Guy Smith

With thanks to the British UFO Research Association, NASA and the Royal Astronomical Society.

CONTENTS

UFOs

A UFO is an Unidentified Flying Object. In the last 50 years, over 200,000 people have reported seeing objects in the sky that experts cannot identify. Societies of enthusiasts called ufologists scan the skies for UFOs. Can so many people be wrong? See what you make of the reports in this book.

Fake or fact?

There are lots of theories about UFOs, and what they could be other than alien spacecraft. Some scientists argue that strange weather conditions produce dazzling lights and shapes in the sky. Others say that UFOs often appear before earthquakes and are caused by the energy in the Earth.

Many researchers think that people who claim to see UFOs have an over-active imagination, or even a certain sort of brain. Fake or fact, people who claim to have seen UFOs usually stick to their stories.

Many UFOs appear to be saucer-shaped, like these.

What UFOs look like

Not all UFOs look like flying saucers. Here are the four most common shapes of UFOs people report, though there are others.

Glowing balls of light like the one on the left make up over 20% of all reported UFOs. The balls are usually orange, yellow or red, or a mixture of all three. They often hover silently above the horizon.

Several glowing balls like this were seen over England in the 1960s.

UFOs looking like large, upside down bowls account for around 8% of cases. Some reports claim that lights flash around the underside rim. In all reports, these UFOs actually land on Earth.

These UFOs seem attracted to metal structures.

UFOs shaped like long, slim tubes also make up around 15% of sightings. Some witnesses speak of tube shapes with rows of lit-up windows along each side and jets of flame coming out of the back.

These are often called cigar-shaped UFOs.

UFOs shaped something like eggs, often giving out a bright white light, account for around 15% of reported sightings. Many witnesses report feeling dizzy and numb while these UFOs are in sight.

These UFOs puzzle experts more than any others.

Open question

It is as difficult to prove that UFOs exist as it is to prove that they do not. The best advice is to "Keep your feet on the ground and your eyes on the skies," as a famous ufologist wrote.

Unsolved puzzles

UFOs are not a new phenomenon. People have been spotting them in the skies for centuries, but until newspapers and television spread information, few people knew about them. According to some researchers, UFOs even visited some of man's earliest civilizations. See what you think.

Help from space?

The pyramids in Egypt were built more than 3,000 years ago, using only very simple tools. They are such an amazing feat of building that some people cannot believe that the Egyptians built them on their own. Did they have help from an alien civilization with technical knowledge far superior to theirs?

There's no evidence to prove this theory, but the pyramids are the source of many unanswered questions...

Star power

One mystery surrounds the way the pyramids seem to line up so precisely with some of the stars in the night sky. Can this be just a coincidence, or were the stars especially important to the pyramid builders for some reason?

The Egyptian pyramids

Space signs

These patterns only take shape when seen from the air.

The Nazca Plateau in Peru, South America, is the site of another possible UFO puzzle. Broad, long lines and huge animal shapes were cut into rock 1,500 years ago by Indian tribes.

Some experts argue that the lines look like a massive airstrip for UFOs. Did the Indians carve the shapes to show passing aliens what lives on this planet?

Dangerous waters

Far more menacing is one theory behind the mysterious disappearance of 120 ships and planes while crossing a triangular area of open sea near the island of Bermuda. The "jinxed" area is now known as The Bermuda Triangle.

Among possible explanations for the disappearances is that aliens are "beaming up" ships and planes to join them in space, so that they can find out about life on Earth.

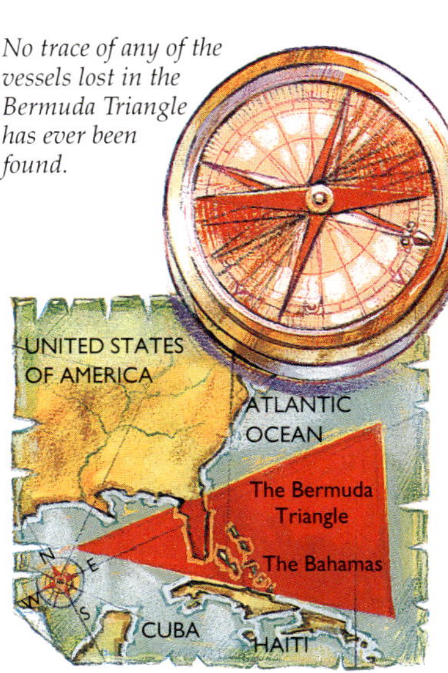

No trace of any of the vessels lost in the Bermuda Triangle has ever been found.

Crop circles

In 1980, reports began coming in about circular patches of grain in English fields being mysteriously flattened. As more flat "crop circles" were found, some argued they were caused by flying saucers landing in the fields.

Strange sights

If you saw an "Unidentified Flying Object", would you report it? Thousands of people have over the last 50 years, though perhaps many more have not. Here are a few UFO sightings.

UFO reports

This UFO, surrounded by a hazy gas, was seen above Richmond in Virginia, USA. It was oval-shaped, and its edges seemed to glow, witnesses said. Around 35m (115ft) long and 10m (30ft) wide, it cruised about 100m (330ft) above the ground.

A policeman and four other witnesses reported spotting a glowing saucer shape in Minnesota, USA, in 1965. It hovered above them in the air, made a whirring noise, and changed from white to orange several times as they watched.

Raphael Jimenez and Manuel Perez reported seeing this glowing saucer flying above them as they drove near Seville in Spain in 1969. They said it swept over the treetops with its lights flashing, and was flying at high speed.

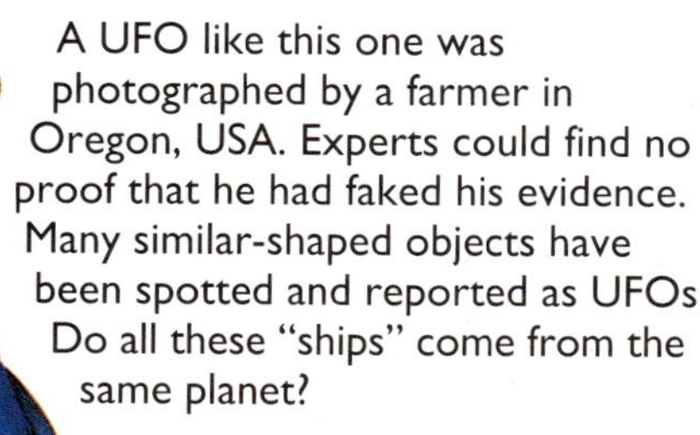

A UFO like this one was photographed by a farmer in Oregon, USA. Experts could find no proof that he had faked his evidence. Many similar-shaped objects have been spotted and reported as UFOs. Do all these "ships" come from the same planet?

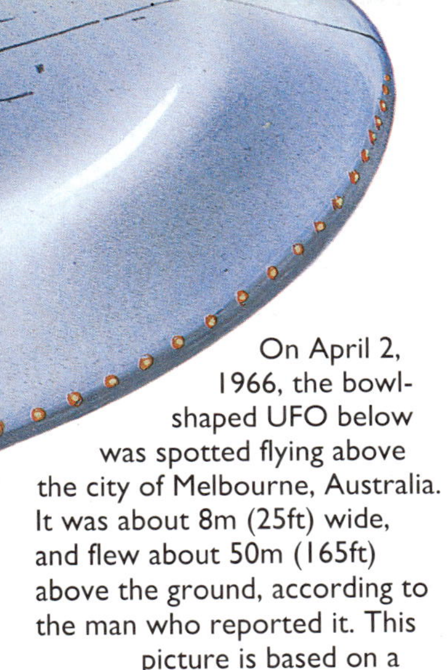

On April 2, 1966, the bowl-shaped UFO below was spotted flying above the city of Melbourne, Australia. It was about 8m (25ft) wide, and flew about 50m (165ft) above the ground, according to the man who reported it. This picture is based on a photograph he took.

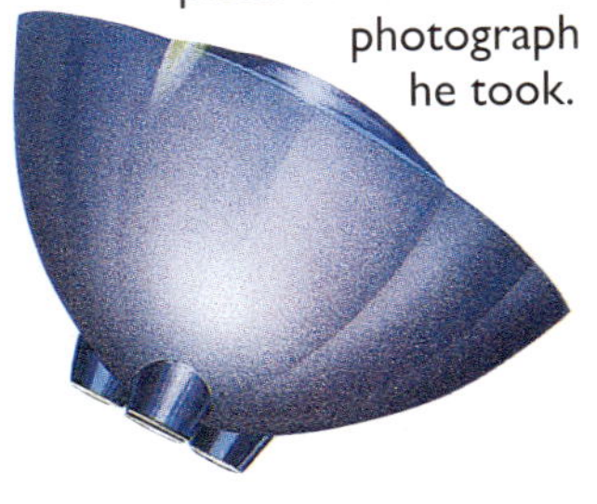

There are two reported sightings of this weird UFO in 1971, in Scotland. The second report states that the craft landed and that three figures got into it just before it took off. The event happened near Loch Ness, but the famous monster was nowhere in sight.

Flying saucers

On June 24, 1947, Kenneth Arnold was alone in his small plane over the Cascade Mountains in the northwest of the United States. Suddenly, he saw nine shining, round, flat objects flying together above the mountains. He described them as flying "like a saucer would if you skipped it across water". They had no tails, and Arnold estimated that they were going almost twice as fast as the speed of sound.

Alien threat?

Arnold was so convinced of what he had seen that an official investigation began into the mysterious "flying saucers". Governments were concerned that they could be threatening to attack Earth. It was the first sighting of a UFO ever to be investigated, but many more were to follow.

You are not alone

The people most likely to encounter a UFO are probably those who constantly scan the sky, or who are up in the air. So perhaps it's not surprising that there are many sightings of UFOs from airport workers and pilots.

Dancing lights

On the night of July 19, 1952, five strange lights appeared in the sky above Washington DC, the American capital. They put on a dazzling display of movements that could be seen from far away. When more of these lights appeared a week later, on July 26, three planes were sent up to investigate. Two pilots could find nothing to report, but the third pilot had an adventure ahead of him.

Surrounded

The pilot of the third jet told astounded listeners back at his base that he could see some

massive white and blue lights ahead. He described the lights as they formed a circle around his plane, flew alongside him for about 15 seconds, then slowly left him. Had they decided not to attack after all, or were they just having a closer look? The mystery remains unsolved.

The Bentwaters Incident

This UFO story begins on the evening of August 13, 1956, as a radar operator was working at an air base in Bentwaters, England. His radar screen picked up an object about 50km (30 miles) away. He calculated that the object was flying at a speed of over 8,000 km (5,000 miles) per hour.

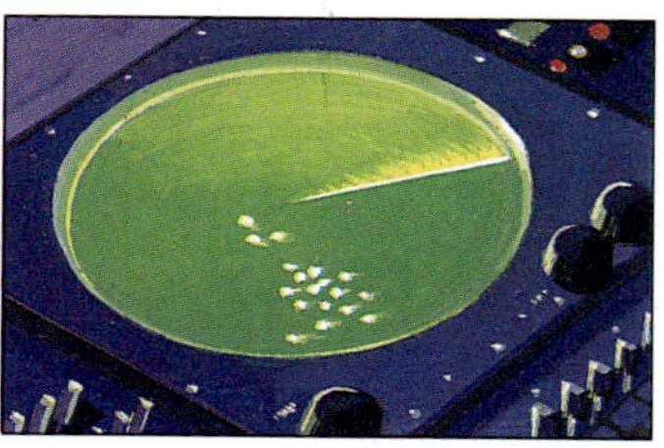

The radar screen then showed a triangular-shaped cluster of about fifteen objects. They seemed to be following three other objects.

Airport visitor

In October 1952, in an airport in Marseilles in southern France, customs officer Gabriel Cachinard was sitting near the aircraft hangars. He noticed a light approaching, then stopping abruptly above the runway. He went nearer to the object and described it as having first a green, then a blue light coming from "windows" around it. Then, Cachinard said sparks shot out from underneath it as it softly sped away.

Sucked up

At precisely 11.02pm on October 18, 1973, a group of people watched a helicopter pass overhead in Mansfield, Ohio. Suddenly, they reported seeing a pale, dome-topped disc with green light streaming from beneath it approaching the helicopter.

Panic

The pilot immediately lost all radio contact. His compass spun wildly as he took the helicopter into a dive, terrified in case he collided with the strange shape. Then, the witnesses below describe seeing the helicopter being quickly sucked up to a height of about 1km (half a mile) underneath the UFO before it flew off, and the terrified pilot regained control.

Later that night, a soldier reported seeing a pinprick of light which stayed still above the base for an hour. A jet sent up to investigate found nothing.

About an hour later, two witnesses saw a "blurred light" stop in the air above the base, then vanish. This light was never identified.

Danger... UFO

Flying has its risks, but pilots do not expect to be chased by UFOs...

Fatal chase

On January 7, 1948, Thomas Mantell piloted one of three planes sent to investigate a strange object seen above Kentucky in the United States. Mantell told base staff that the thing "appeared to be metallic". The other two pilots returned to base, but Mantell followed the object higher. Mantell's wrecked plane was later found over 135km (80 miles) away from his base. Had a UFO led him to his death?

UFO alert

Many people reported seeing a bright light in the sky over an airbase near Tehran, Iran, one September night in 1976. Around 2am, a jet took off to investigate. As it approached, the light flashed blue, green, red and orange and shot out a smaller object. This object followed the plane into a dive.

Earth probe?

Then the object sped back to the larger ship, which shot out a second object. This was never found. Could it have been a kind of exploratory device?

Golden ball

On January 11, 1973, a US Air Force jet crashed over England, having reported electrical interference. Later, a piece of film shot by Peter Day in the area of the crash revealed a mysterious orange egg-shaped light moving just above the ground. Other witnesses said that the light was rotating, and that its top was domed. An investigation found that the jet had started having engine trouble at exactly the time Day had filmed the glowing ball.

Hide and seek

The crew of a US Air Force jet survived being chased by a UFO. On June 17, 1957, an unknown flying craft followed them for over 1,000km (620 miles), dodging on and off radar screens. The UFO seemed to be playing hide and seek with the jet, a game that even the plane's up-to-date technical equipment could not win.

Empty space?

The astronauts on board the space flights of the 1960s and 1970s returned with many tales of strange objects and mysterious lights. The crew of Apollo 11 in 1969 reported seeing a shape "like an open suitcase" flying near them. The astronauts of Apollo 12 saw something flashing alongside their spacecraft before it flew off very fast into space.

Mystery

In June 1965, James McDivitt, an astronaut on board Gemini 4, saw an object with "big arms sticking out of it" float past his spacecraft. He took photographs, but was unable to find them later.

Although these stories are as difficult to prove as any other UFO sighting, astronauts certainly have a ringside seat on anything that is going on in space.

Close encounters

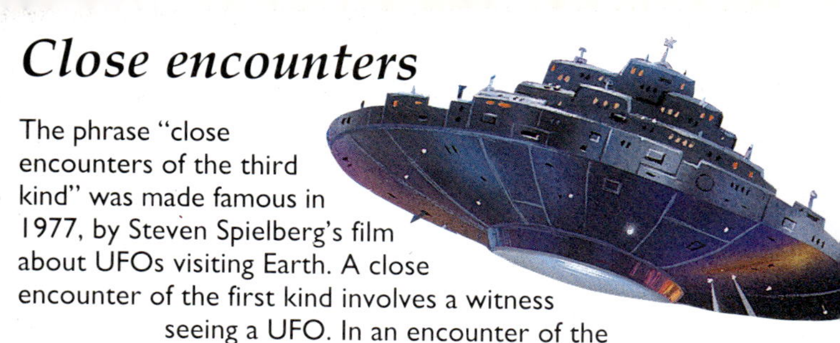

The phrase "close encounters of the third kind" was made famous in 1977, by Steven Spielberg's film about UFOs visiting Earth. A close encounter of the first kind involves a witness seeing a UFO. In an encounter of the second kind, the UFO leaves evidence, such as scorch marks, a crater, or scars on a witness. Encounters of the third and fourth kind are described on pages 16 to19.

Now you see it...

A famous close encounter of the first kind happened on January 20, 1988, on the road between the Australian cities of Perth and Adelaide. Faye Knowles and her three grown-up sons were driving through the night and the incident took place at around 4am.

Ghastly game

The family later told scientists that a pale yellow balloon-shaped mass had moved around their car as if it was playing with them. The Knowles sat in their car, too scared to get out or even to scream.

Strange feelings

Soon they were sure that the "thing" was directly above them, as it was vibrating and humming loudly. They reported a horrible smell in the car and a fine, milky mist floating in through an open window.

The ordeal ends

Finally, their car was lifted off the ground and dropped again. Only when the light mass had disappeared did they dare to drive on. Nothing was proved, but investigators found dents in the car's roof, which was covered with a strange dust.

Egg encounter

A close encounter of the second kind happened one night in Baltimore, Maryland, USA. On October 26, 1958, two motorists approached a bridge. They saw an egg-shaped object hovering above it. Suddenly, the object gave out a dazzling light and a wave of intense heat. As it roared into the sky, the motorists felt the heat burn their faces as they watched. Doctors later found that both mens' faces looked as if they had been burned by radiation.

The two men reported that the egg was glowing.

Scary stories

Three scary encounters happened within 24 hours in France, on October 20 and 21, 1954.

On the rainy night of the 20th, an oval light approached Roger Reveille, then flew up and vanished. It was so hot that it turned rain to steam. The spot it had hovered above was dry, but the grass around was wet.

On the same day, a Mr. Schoubrenner reported seeing an upside-down cone-shape on the road in Sarrebourg. His muscles were frozen. Somehow, he braked and watched as a soft glow poured out of the disappearing cone.

On October 21, a man and his three-year-old child saw a red and orange light on the road in Pouzou. He said he felt electric shocks, his car stalled and his child began to cry. Then the light slowly vanished.

Aliens aboard

A close encounter of the third kind involves a human witness seeing an alien creature. This forms the dramatic climax of Steven Spielberg's famous film *Close Encounters of the Third Kind*. Some UFO researchers have now added another kind of encounter to the list, an encounter of the fourth kind. You can read more about these on pages 18-19.

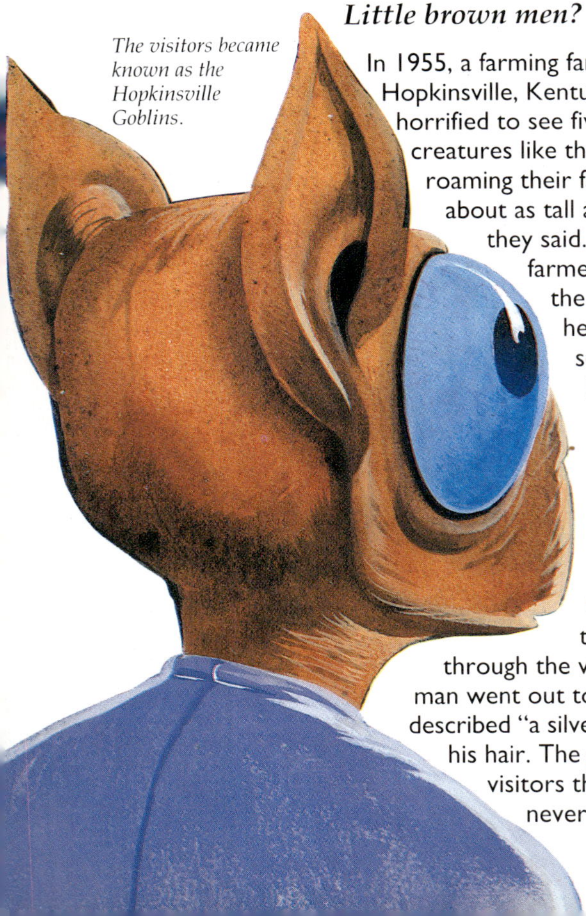

The visitors became known as the Hopkinsville Goblins.

Little brown men?

In 1955, a farming family in Hopkinsville, Kentucky, USA, were horrified to see five golden-brown creatures like the one shown here roaming their farm. Each one was about as tall as a small child, they said. The terrified farmer shot at one of the creatures and heard a metallic sound as the bullet hit it, but the alien seemed unhurt.

Gentle goblins

Later, when the family were sitting inside their farmhouse, one of the aliens peered in through the window. When one man went out to investigate, he described "a silvery hand" brushing his hair. The gentle-seeming visitors then vanished, never to return.

Roadside mystery

A famous encounter of the third kind was reported by a police officer in 1964. It has never been satisfactorily explained away by experts.

On the night of April 24, Lonnie Zamora was on duty near Socorro in New Mexico, USA. As he chased a speeding motorist, he became aware of a strange blue light and a roaring noise coming from the sky. He drove toward the light and saw an oval-shaped, silver object on four metal feet "parked" beside the road. Officer Zamora then reported seeing two small figures dressed in white moving around the object.

As soon as the little figures heard Zamora's approach, they fled into the oval shape. A roar filled the desert air, followed by a blue flame as the object took off and disappeared.

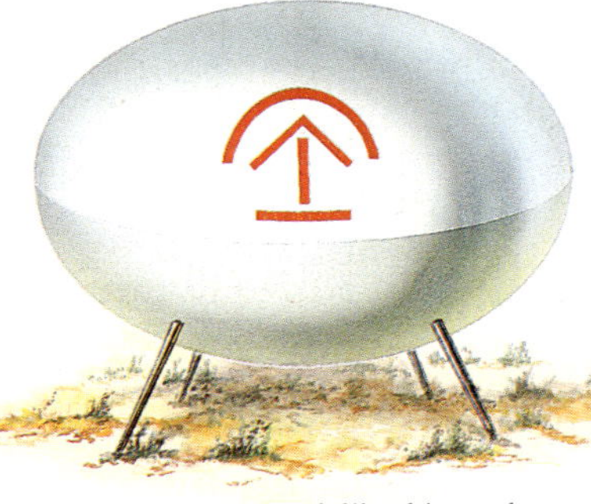

Zamora saw a mark like this on the side of the oval UFO. No airforce on Earth has ever used anything like it.

Evidence?

Zamora admitted that he was terrified and experts were impressed with his story when they later interviewed him.

Investigators visited the site of the encounter and discovered four wedge-shaped marks in the ground and an area of burned bushes around them. Had the marks been made by the UFO's four legs and the bushes burned as it took off, just as Zamora had described?

Icy encounter

Close encounters of the third kind seem to take place under all kinds of unusual circumstances. Gampiere Monguzzi took this photo while trekking across the Bernina glacier. He said that the figure to the left of the craft was an alien.

Abducted by aliens

Reports of close encounters of the fourth kind involve being abducted by aliens. Many witnesses tend to have very active imaginations, according to tests. This is enough to make some experts doubt their stories.

Amazing trip

There have been several reported encounters of the fourth kind in South America. In the first such case, in 1957, a Brazilian farmworker called Antonio Villas Boas said that aliens landed in a field and forced him to go on board a UFO.

A female alien beckoned him to follow her and said she would later have his baby up in space, Boas said. As news of this astounding report spread, many more soon followed.

Space map

Several encounters of the fourth kind have been reported in the United States. One story concerns Betty and Barney Hill, who were driving through New Hampshire in 1961.

The couple said that they had been abducted by aliens. Barney was able to draw a sketch of the inside of the UFO they said they had been taken on board. Betty spoke of meeting aliens aboard the UFO and said that their leader had shown her a star chart. He told her that the solid lines marked trading routes that their ship followed between alien settlements, and that the dotted lines were expedition routes. Whether the Hills invented such details remains an unsolved mystery.

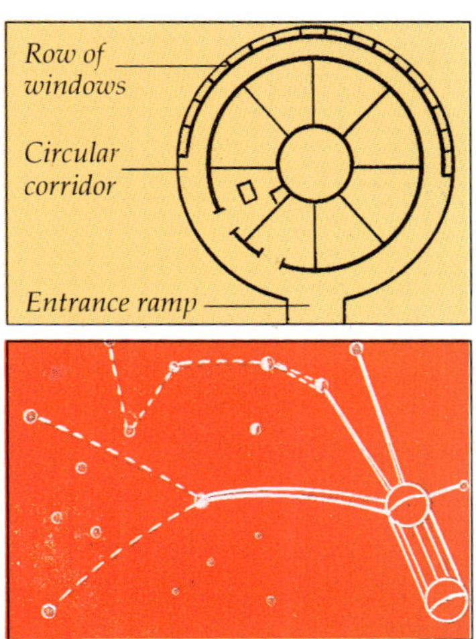

Balls of light

On October 15, 1979, Luli Oswald, a pianist, was driving along the coast at Ponta Negra in Brazil. She describes seeing a light rising from the sea with a tower of water beneath it. Three balls of light rolled toward her car. She became unconscious...

Oswald came around two hours later, farther down the road. She was desperate to know what had happened in those two hours. She agreed to be hypnotized to help her remember, and described her car being "beamed up" into a UFO. Dwarf-like creatures examined her and told her that they came from near the planet Neptune. She recalled nothing else until she regained consciousness in her car.

Mistaken identity

As many as 95% of reported sightings of UFOs are mistakes. Many of these are probably caused by people seeing real aircraft, but from unusual angles or in a strange light. Some aircraft have very weird shapes, though. Many people might be amazed if they saw some of these machines flying overhead.

Flying pancake

This German Second World War prototype aircraft was called the *Fliegender Pfannkuchen*, which means "flying pancake".

Avro Avrocar

This amazing machine proved that saucer-shaped aircraft don't fly very well, at least not when human engineers build them. It was built in Canada in 1959, but it did not hover in the air or take off vertically as its designers had hoped. It wobbled so much that it had to be tied to the ground with steel cables and only ever hovered about 1m (3ft) off the ground. Perhaps alien engineers have solved these problems in ways that humans have not yet discovered.

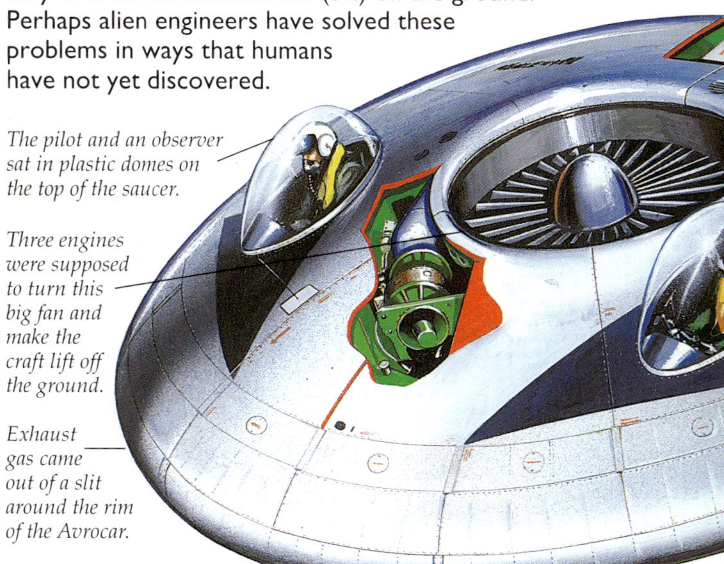

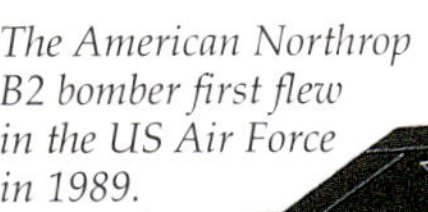

The American Northrop B2 bomber first flew in the US Air Force in 1989.

Night spies

These incredible-looking planes are called stealth planes. They are designed to creep up on things without being seen. Their shape helps to confuse enemy radar systems, and they are painted black to make them hard to spot at night. Their wings are even covered with a substance that makes radar signals bounce back, so that the planes are "invisible" to enemy radar trying to track them.

This is the Lockheed F117A. It first flew in 1981 but no one knew anything about it until seven years later.

Egg-shaped spy

This is a remote-controlled spy helicopter, called the Westland Wisp. It is designed to be carried on the back of a jeep. A pilot sitting safely in the jeep can instruct it to spy on enemy troops as it flies over them. Its egg-like shape and four feet do look remarkably like many reported UFOs...

The Wisp's two spinning rotor blades lift it into the sky.

Space, the final frontier

Man began exploring space in 1957 when Russia launched a rocket called a sputnik. On July 20, 1969, an American spacecraft landed on the Moon. Today, many spaceprobes are journeying through space, sending back information.

Spaceprobes

Spaceprobes are unmanned, and travel through space piloted by computers. This means they can stay in space far longer than astronauts. None have found any signs of life in space... yet.

Mariner 10 was launched from the US in November 1973. It flew above the surface of the planet Mercury.

In August 1976, the Viking 2 Lander touched down on Mars. It dug up soil to be tested for signs of life, but scientists have yet to find any.

In September 1979, Pioneer 11 took amazing photographs of Saturn and its rings. Astronomers had first been puzzled by them in 1631.

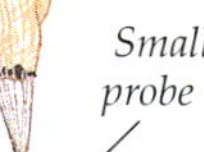

Small probe

A probe called Galileo is currently scanning Jupiter, taking photographs. One part of the probe is sinking through its atmosphere, taking measurements.

Space message

In 1974, a radio telescope in Puerto Rico, South America, beamed a coded message out into space. It briefly described life on Earth. If anyone picks up this message, their reply won't reach us for thousands of years.

Coded message

Mysterious Mars

There are deep channels on the the planet Mars. Some 19th century astronomers thought that they were dug by Martians.

A Martian?

In 1898, a writer called H. G. Wells wrote a book, *The War of the Worlds*, describing a Martian invasion of Earth. When it was read on the radio in America in 1938, many people thought it was really happening, and panicked.

Mars

Life in space

Many scientists hope to build bases out in space for humans to live in, on the Moon or Mars for instance. Here is an imaginary base on a planet without oxygen in its atmosphere. Would you like to live here?

A starship leaves for Earth and other planets.

These domes are filled with oxygen for the people at the base to breathe.

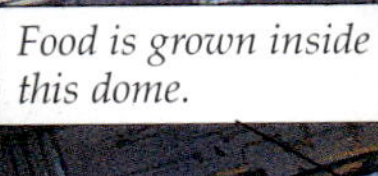

This tunnel runs between the domes.

Look again...

According to organizations that monitor UFOs, most people report puzzling lights in the sky rather than flying saucers. Some of these "UFOs" turn out to be the flashing lights of aircraft, many are satellites, some are planets or stars twinkling. These are called IFOs, or Identifiable Flying Objects.

There are a surprising number of other things that fool people into thinking they are UFOs. Some of these are shown below. Would they fool you?

A car is approaching the top of the hill from the other side. The beams from its headlights are reflected in the clouds above the hill.

A flock of geese flew over the city of Lubbock, Texas, USA in 1951. The city lights were reflected on the underside of their white bodies, like this.

When air rises above hills, several amazing clouds might appear, in a formation such as this. These clouds are called lenticular (lens-shaped) clouds.

The long, ribbon-like exhaust trails from aircraft sometimes get broken up by the wind into separate tubular objects like the ones shown here.

Ships in need of help send up bright flares which sink slowly to the ground. Their controlled fall to Earth might look like a very careful UFO landing.

Rocks and stones from space (called meteors) burn up as they fall across the sky. A group, or belt, of meteors crosses the Earth's orbit regularly.

When the Moon is partly covered by clouds, it can be mistaken for a strange object. Up to 5% of reported UFOs turn out to be the Moon.

The Sun can shine through thin clouds but it can look like a hazy ball as it does so. This unusual effect can make people think it is a UFO.

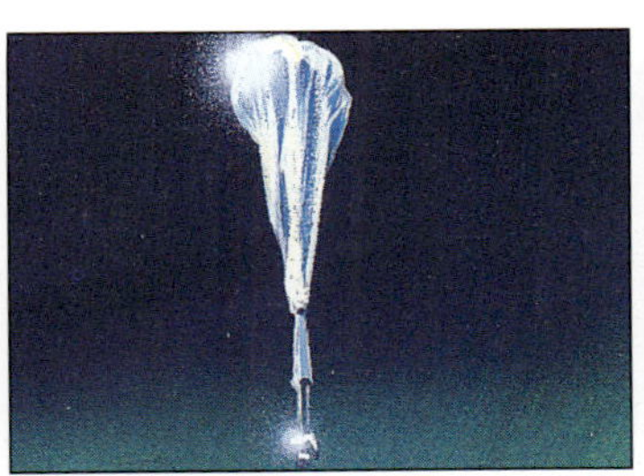

Huge balloons made of a metallic fabric carry scientific instruments high up into the atmosphere. Their eerie pale shape can be hard to identify.

One UFO investigation concluded that a small, shiny shape reported as a UFO was really an owl that had eaten fungi that glowed in the dark.

Skywatching

Scanning the skies for UFOs is often called skywatching. Groups of ufologists mount skywatches to investigate reported sightings, or in areas known to be UFO "hotspots". There is no guarantee that they will spot a UFO, but following these guidelines make it more likely.

Where to skywatch

The best place to spot a UFO is probably on a hill, to get a clear view. It is a good idea to go outside a town or city. Street lights and car headlights reflect on the sky and tall buildings block the view in built-up areas.

When to skywatch

You might see UFOs better at night. More than 75% of UFOs are spotted between 10pm and 7am: 3am seems to be a particularly busy time. Skywatching at night should only ever be done in properly organized groups, run by adults.

Does the weather matter?

The skies are clearest after a spell of rainy weather, so skywatchers check weather forecasts. Stormy weather can produce strange-looking clouds, too (see pages 24-25), so skywatchers try to avoid organizing a trip in these difficult conditions.

Recognizing a UFO

If skywatchers spot something, they check all the things it could be, other than a UFO. There are some possibilities on pages 24-25. The most common shapes of reported UFOs are on pages 4-5. If the object resembles one of these, they may investigate further.

UFO Report Form

Skywatchers often note down everything they see on forms like this one.

UFO REPORT FORM

1. Location ....
2. Date ....
3. Time ....
4. Witnesses present at skywatch
....
5. Weather conditions ....
6. Exact duration of UFO sighting
....
7. Sketch of UFO
8. Details of lights, movement and sounds made by UFO..........................
....
....
9. Was the UFO photographed? ....
10. Further action ....
....

Fact or fiction?

It is easy to fake a photograph of a UFO, but not so easy to fool the experts. What do you make of this photograph: fake or the real thing? (Answer on page 32.)

What you need

Dedicated UFO-spotters have lots of equipment, but you really only need a few basic things to make a skywatch enjoyable.

1. It is vital to note down everything seen during the skywatch, so notepads and pens are vital. You could use a UFO Report Form like the one on this page.

2. Times of any activity in the sky must be written down, so a reliable watch is essential. "UFOs" might be passing planes, but this can only be proved if times can later be checked with the airport.

3. A camera is useful, preferably loaded with film that is designed to take pictures in dim light. Flashes will not light up an object far away in the sky and may ruin pictures, so do not use a flash.

UFO photofile

Thousands of people have taken photographs of UFOs. Although many of them have been explained, many more remain a mystery. Here are four photographs of reported UFOs. See what you make of them.

This is probably the first UFO photograph ever taken. It was snapped at the port of Drobach in Normandy on July 27, 1907.

Harry Hauxler took this photograph at Oberwesel in Germany, in August 1964. The UFO appears to be spinning above the town.

This astounding photograph was taken at San José de Valderas in Spain, on June 1, 1967. Compare it to the story on page 17.

This picture was taken by Francis Walters in November 1987, at Gulf Breeze, Florida in the USA.

Draw your own aliens

Nobody can be sure what creatures from other planets look like. Four very different alien faces are shown on this page. They have some human characteristics, and some more unusual ones. Try using these ideas to create an alien of your own. Nobody can tell you your portrait isn't accurate!

Where to start

The three small pictures next to each alien show you in what order the parts of each face were drawn. It might help you to follow these stages as you draw.

This alien's face looks strong but thoughtful. Respectable clothing and firm features such as a prominent chin make him look mature. Would you trust him?

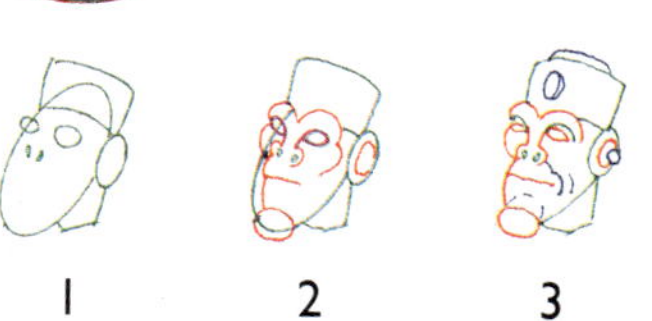

Sharp teeth, slimy reptile skin and a viciously pointed beak combine to make this alien look mean and menacing. Slit eyes add a nasty sneer.

1 2 3

Are the hooks above this alien's face for attack or to defend herself? Her skin looks strangely oily, though her mouth is smiling. She could be more cunning than she first appears.

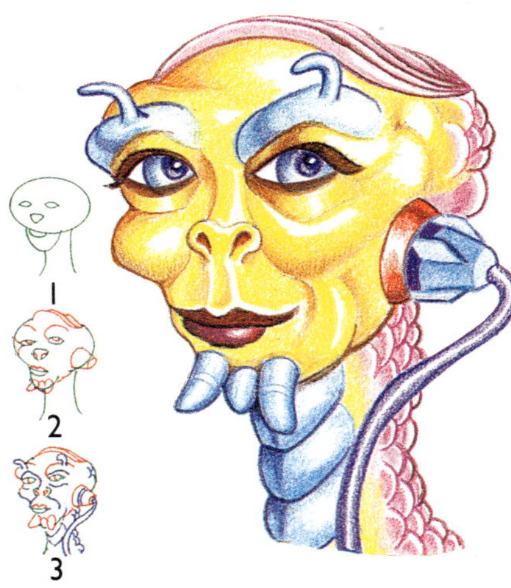

This alien means business. He wears warlike clothes and has razor-sharp teeth. His single, fiery eye looks very unpleasant. His huge mouth and sweaty skin are not very attractive, either.

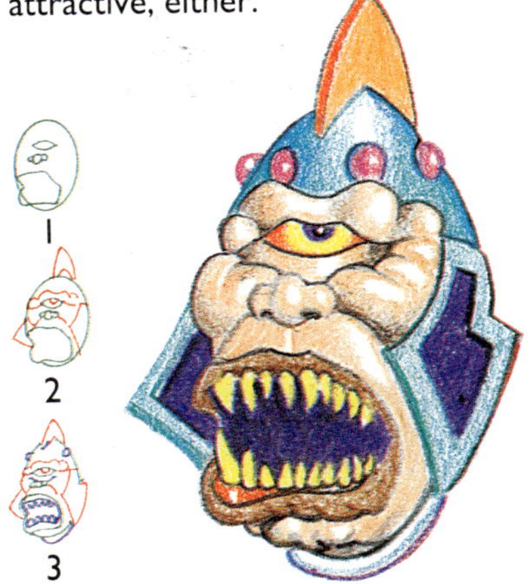

Alien skin

You can give your alien a skin to suit its character. A smooth complexion will make an alien seem gentler than one covered in hideous bristly warts. Try these techniques as you draw your aliens.

Gouache or poster paint is thick, and can make skin look tough. It's good for creating dark shadow, too.

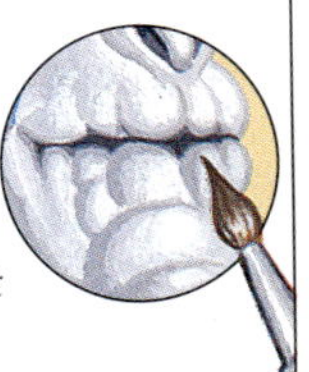

Create smooth skin by using watery paint. When dry, add streaks of white to make it look wet and slippery.

Pencil crayons make skin look soft as they blend together well. Don't press too hard as you use them.

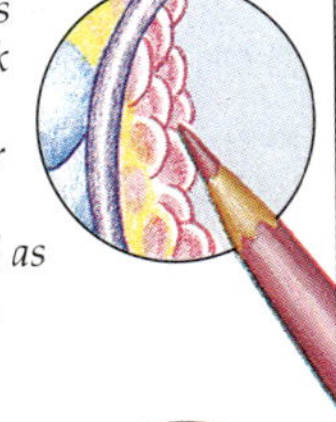

Wax crayons are good for rough-textured skin. Several crayons used on top of each other create new shades, too.

Index

Answer to question on page 27: This "UFO" is a saucepan lid, thrown into the air by a photographer lying down. Because the photo was taken from a hill, the lid looks as if it is flying higher than the city buildings in the distance.

Acknowledgements
Tim Dedopulos BSC, Alan Fossey, Alan Smith, Aerial Phenomena Research Organization, British UFO Documentation Centre, Flying Saucer Review, George Adamski Foundation, Norman Oliver, Robert Digby, Timothy Good.
Photographs on pages 17, 28 and 29: Images Colour Library

First published in 1996 by Usborne Publishing Ltd, Usborne House, 83-85 Saffron Hill, London EC1N 8RT, England.

First published in America in March 1997. UE
Printed in Italy